For everyone who has ever wanted to be a princess–*M.H.*
To En-Szu, a princess in her own right–*C.V.W & Y.H.*

DIAL BOOKS FOR YOUNG READERS
A division of Penguin Young Readers Group
Published by The Penguin Group
Penguin Group (USA) Inc., 375 Hudson Street, New York, NY 10014, U.S.A.
Penguin Group (Canada), 90 Eglinton Avenue East, Suite 700, Toronto, Ontario, Canada M4P 2Y3 (a division of Pearson Penguin Canada Inc.)
Penguin Books Ltd, 80 Strand, London WC2R 0RL, England
Penguin Ireland, 25 St. Stephen's Green, Dublin 2, Ireland (a division of Penguin Books Ltd)
Penguin Group (Australia), 250 Camberwell Road, Camberwell, Victoria 3124, Australia (a division of Pearson Australia Group Pty Ltd)
Penguin Books India Pvt Ltd, 11 Community Centre, Panchsheel Park, New Delhi - 110 017, India
Penguin Group (NZ), Cnr Airborne and Rosedale Roads, Albany, Auckland 1310, New Zealand (a division of Pearson New Zealand Ltd)
Penguin Books (South Africa) (Pty) Ltd, 24 Sturdee Avenue, Rosebank, Johannesburg 2196, South Africa
Penguin Books Ltd, Registered Offices: 80 Strand, London WC2R 0RL, England

First published in the United States 2008 by
Dial Books for Young Readers
Published in Great Britain 2007 by
Frances Lincoln Children's Books, 4 Torriano Mews,
Torriano Avenue, London NW5 2RZ
www.franceslincoln.com

Text set in Caslon Book
Printed in China
3 5 7 9 10 8 6 4 2

Library of Congress Cataloging-in-Publication Data is available upon request

Princess Grace

by Mary Hoffman

illustrated by Cornelius Van Wright
and Ying-Hwa Hu

Dial Books for Young Readers

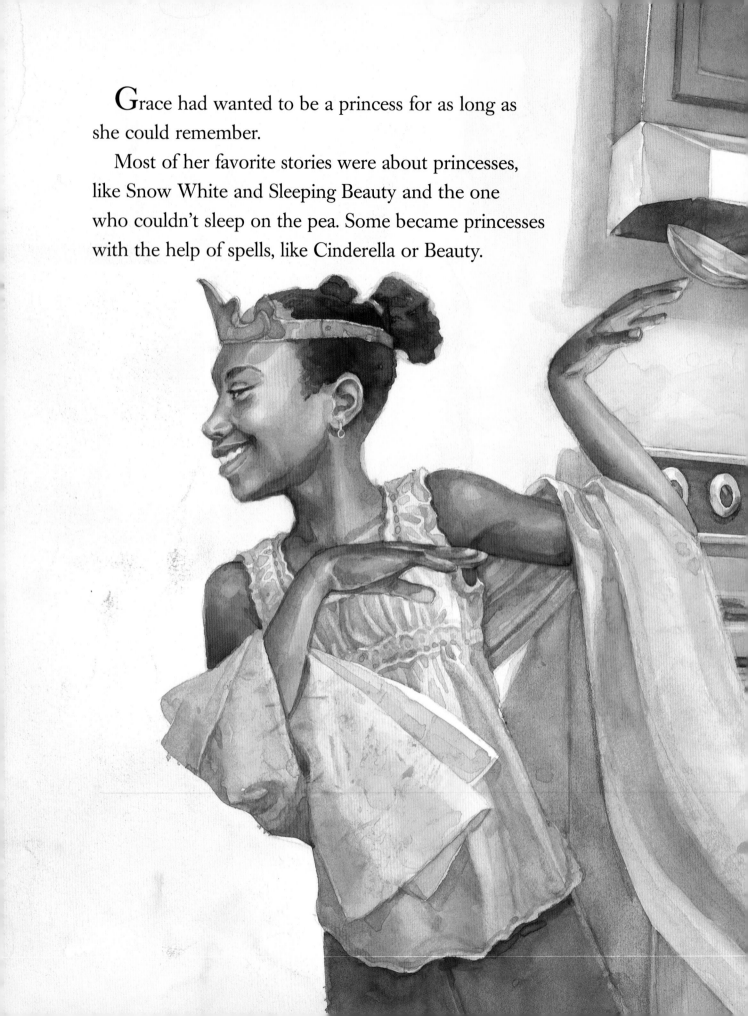

Grace had wanted to be a princess for as long as she could remember.

Most of her favorite stories were about princesses, like Snow White and Sleeping Beauty and the one who couldn't sleep on the pea. Some became princesses with the help of spells, like Cinderella or Beauty.

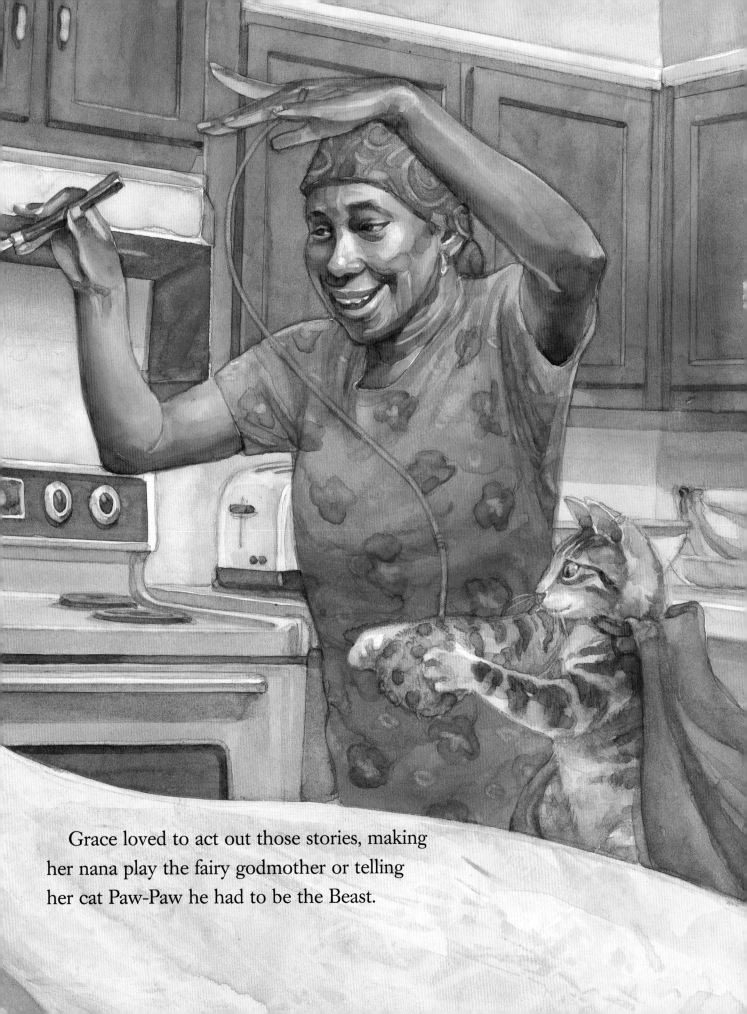

Grace loved to act out those stories, making
her nana play the fairy godmother or telling
her cat Paw-Paw he had to be the Beast.

So imagine Grace's excitement at school, when her teacher
announced the annual community festival. Every year girls
from all the local schools got to be queens in the parade, and
this year there were going to be two princesses!

"At this year's parade, our float will be extra-special," said
the teacher. "Our queen, who has already been chosen from the
top year, had the idea to pick two princesses from our class."

Well, after that, all the girls were twirling in
imaginary ballgowns and saying that they were
bound to be the parade princess.

Especially Natalie.

"My daddy always calls me his princess," she said.
"So I'm used to being one."

This made Grace sad for two reasons. She didn't like
Natalie and she didn't have a daddy of her own.
At least not one who lived with her.

The boys were pretty disgusted with the whole idea.

"Princesses are boring," said Kester.

Grace rushed home very excited to tell Ma and Nana the news.

"So can I be a princess, Ma?" she asked. "And will you make me a costume, Nana?"

"Of course, honey," said Nana. "If you can tell me what a princess wears, I can try to make it."

"And of course you can dress up as a princess, Grace," said Ma. "But that doesn't mean you'll get chosen in the parade."

So Grace rushed off to get out all her storybooks to see if she could find out what princesses wear.

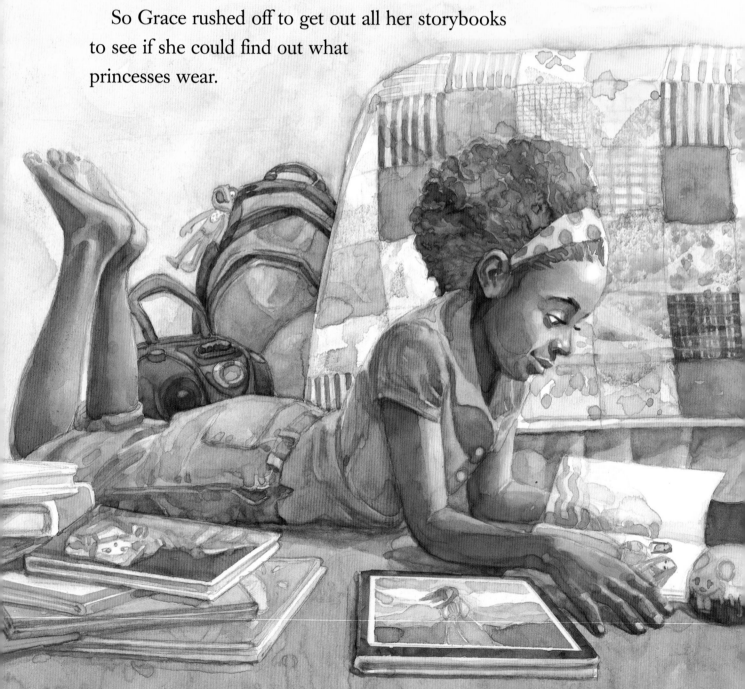

Her best friends Aimee and Maria came around to help. They didn't want to be princesses as much as Grace did, because Maria didn't like being looked at and Aimee didn't think her mother would have time to make her a costume.

"It must be pink and floaty,
with a train," said Grace.
"And a crown," said Aimee.
"And a wand," said Maria.
"No," said Grace. "That's fairies."
"Wings then?" suggested Maria.
"Fairies again," said Grace.
"Or angels," said Aimee.

"So what am I making?" asked Nana, confused.
"I don't know if it's a dress for a Christmas tree fairy
or a bridal gown."

"It's a bit like all of those, I think," said Grace.
"Oh, I don't know. It must be very pretty."

"There's more than one way to be pretty," said Nana.

"I suppose it depends what she does," said Aimee.

"I don't know," said Grace. "What does a princess do, Nana?"

"You tell me, darling," said Nana.

But nobody could, except for wearing beautiful clothes
and looking pretty.

"That doesn't sound so interesting," said Grace.
She liked having things to do. "Maybe Kester was right."

"You know what?" said Nana. "I think maybe you've been
reading the wrong stories. Why don't you ask your teacher?"

So that's what Grace did.

Her teacher took it very seriously and came back to class with a whole lot of stories about interesting princesses.

There were real ones like Amina of Nigeria, who led warriors into battle and built walls around all the villages, and Pin-Yang of China, who started a women's army.

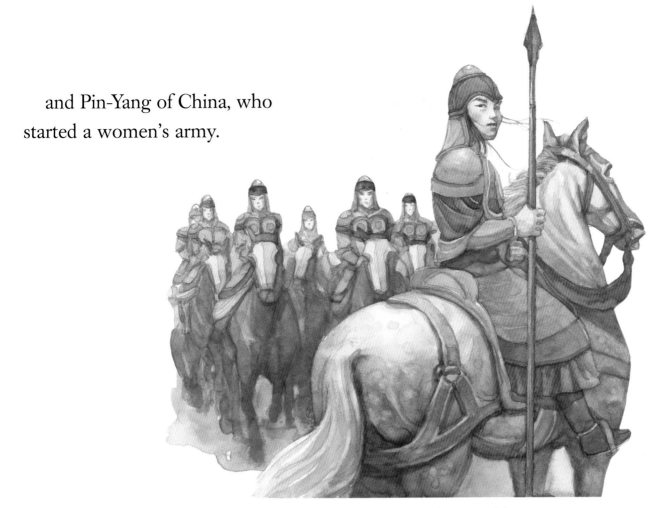

"Wow," said Grace, surprised. "They sound more like soldiers than princesses."

"They wouldn't wear anything pretty while they were fighting," said Natalie. "I don't want to be that kind of princess."

But their teacher had found modern princesses too, who were sportswomen or scientists or artists—one had even been a spy!

"That's a bit more like it," said Kester. "You could be one like that, Grace."

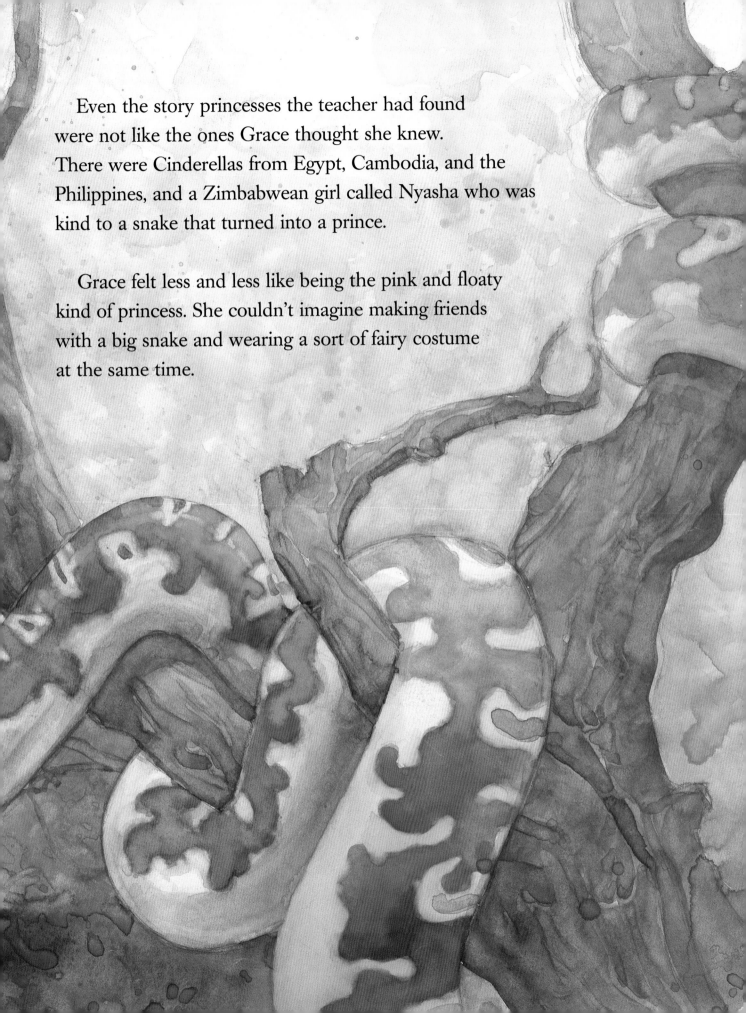

Even the story princesses the teacher had found
were not like the ones Grace thought she knew.
There were Cinderellas from Egypt, Cambodia, and the
Philippines, and a Zimbabwean girl called Nyasha who was
kind to a snake that turned into a prince.

Grace felt less and less like being the pink and floaty
kind of princess. She couldn't imagine making friends
with a big snake and wearing a sort of fairy costume
at the same time.

"Can't there be princes in the parade?" asked Raj at lunch.
"Why does it have to be just princesses?"

"And why just the pink and pretty sort?" said Grace.
"Can't we have some of these other kinds from other countries?"

"You've changed your tune, Grace," said their teacher.
"I thought you loved fairytale princesses."

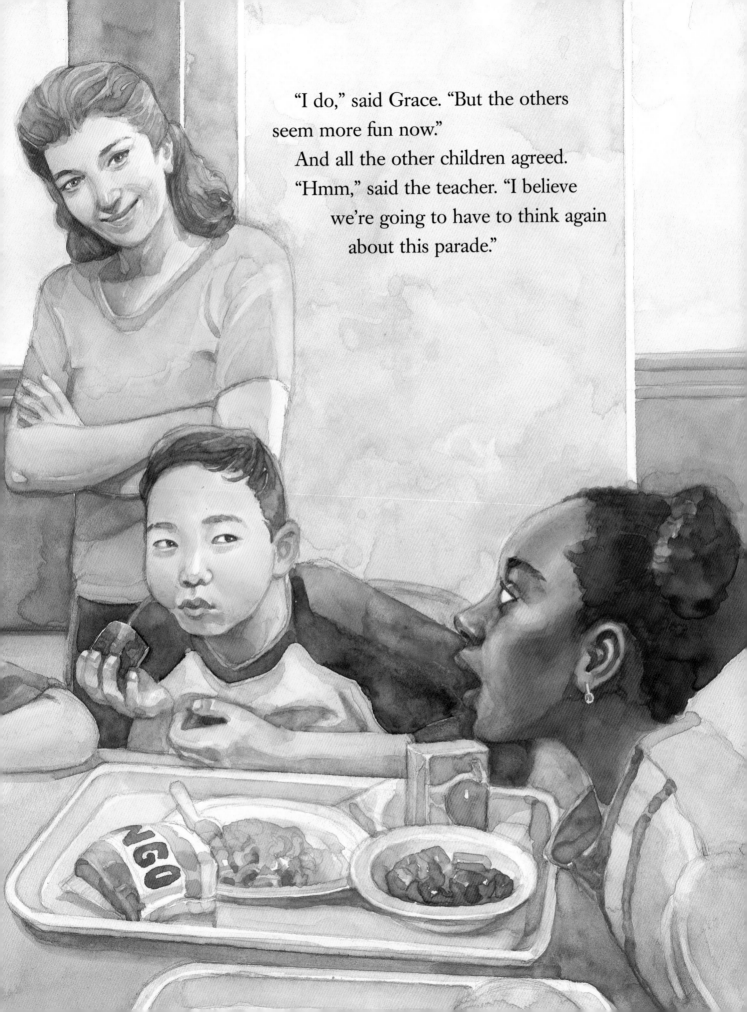

"I do," said Grace. "But the others
seem more fun now."
And all the other children agreed.
"Hmm," said the teacher. "I believe
we're going to have to think again
about this parade."

The moms and dads and grannies and babysitters
all chatted at the school gates. And the word soon
went around about princes and princesses.

"You need to decide, Grace," said Nana. "Have you
made up your mind what sort of princess you want to be?"

"The kind that has adventures," said Grace.
"And I'd like to be an African one. Is there one from
The Gambia? Can you find me a story?"

"Hold on," said Ma. "Have you been chosen yet?"

"Oh," said Grace. "No, I haven't. I forgot about that."

"No harm in being prepared," said Nana. "Do you know
any Gambian princess stories?"

"You could ring your papa," said Ma. "He might know."
But Grace's papa didn't know any, nor did his wife, Jatou.
"It doesn't matter, Grace," said Nana. "I could use some of that Kente cloth we brought back from The Gambia and make you robes fit for a princess."
"It won't be pink," said Ma. "Will you still like it, Grace?"
"There's more than one way of being pretty," said Grace.

On the day of the parade Grace's school had
the most interesting float of all. But it was
a bit crowded because of all the Japanese
and African and Spanish princes and princesses.
The whole class had been chosen.

Maria didn't mind being looked at because
she wasn't the only one, and Nana
had made a dress for Aimee too.

Raj was a Hindu prince and Kester was a sort of English knight. Natalie was like a Christmas tree fairy in a pink and floaty dress.

But Grace didn't want to be that kind of princess anymore.
She was enjoying her West African Kente robes.

"Are you happy?" called Nana.

"Yes," said Grace. "I feel like a proper princess—
ready for an adventure."

Princesses come in all shapes and sizes.
As well as the traditional European stories, like Sleeping Beauty,
there are many versions of Cinderella:
for example, the Egyptian Rhodopis with her golden slippers,
Abadeha from the Philippines, and the Cambodian Princess Angkat.
The story of Nyasha and the snake is most easily found in
John Steptoe's *Mufaro's Beautiful Daughters*.

The real-life princess Amina lived in Zaria (now Nigeria)
in the sixteenth century and Pin-Yang was a princess in China
over a thousand years ago. Princess Noor Inayat Khan of Hyderabad
(now in Andhra Pradesh) was shot by the Germans
in Dachau in World War II for being a spy in France.

Kente cloth is made by the Asante peoples of Ghana
and the Ewe peoples of Ghana and Togo,
and is the best known of all African textiles.
Asante kente (known as "the cloth of kings"), which Grace wears,
is identified by its dazzling, multicolored patterns
of geometric shapes and bold designs.